This **F**rog book belongs
belongs to:

....

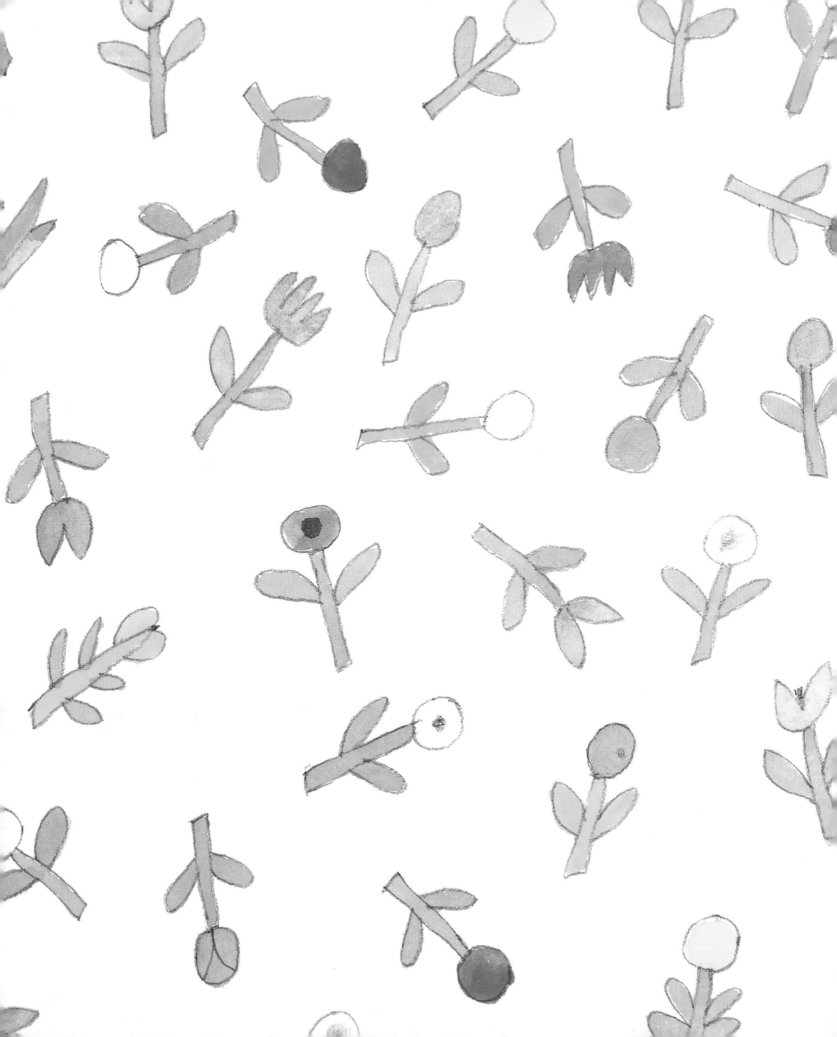

This paperback edition first published in 2014 by Andersen Press Ltd.

20 Vauxhall Bridge Road, London SW1V 2SA.

First published in Great Britain in 1991 by Andersen Press Ltd.

Published in Australia by Random House Australia Pty.,

20 Alfred Street, Milsons Point, Sydney, NSW 2061.

Copyright © Max Velthuijs Foundation, 1991

The rights of Max Velthuijs to be identified as the author and illustrator

of this work have been asserted by him in accordance with the

Copyright, Designs and Patents Act, 1988.

Colour separated in Switzerland by Photolitho AG, Zürich.

Printed and bound in China by Foshan Zhao Rong printing Co., Ltd

10   9   8   7   6   5   4   3   2   1

British Library Cataloguing in Publication Data available.

ISBN 978 1 78344 146 4

Frog
and the Birdsong

Max Velthuijs

Andersen Press

It was a beautiful autumn day.
Pig was picking ripe apples in the orchard . . .

. . . when along came Frog. He looked worried.

"I've found something," he said.
"What is it?" asked Pig.

"Come with me and I'll show you," replied Frog.

And they set off together.
Pig felt nervous.

When they arrived at a clearing, Frog pointed
at the ground.
"Look," he said. "There's something wrong
with this blackbird. He's not moving."

"He's asleep," said Pig.

Just then, Duck arrived.

"What's the matter?" she asked with concern.
"Has there been an accident?"
"Ssh, he's asleep," said Frog.
But Duck thought he looked ill.

At that moment Hare was walking through the woods. He saw from a distance that something was going on and joined the others.

He knelt beside the bird and said, "He's dead."
"Dead," said Frog. "What's that?"
Hare pointed up at the blue sky.

"Everything dies," he said.
"Even us?" asked Frog.
Hare wasn't sure.
"Perhaps, when we're old," he said.

"We must bury him," said Hare, "over there,
at the bottom of the hill."

Together, they made a stretcher and carried
the bird into the meadow.

They dug a deep hole in the ground.

"All his life he sang beautifully for us," said Hare.
"Now he has earned his rest."

Very carefully they laid the dead bird in the hole.
Frog threw flowers all around it and then they
covered the bird with earth.

Finally they put a beautiful stone on top. It was very peaceful. There was not a sound - not even one note of birdsong.

They were all very moved and went quietly on their way. Suddenly, Frog ran ahead.

"Let's play catch," he shouted excitedly.
"Pig, you're IT."

They played and laughed until sunset.

"Isn't life wonderful?" said Frog.

The tired friends set off happily for home.
As they passed the bottom of the hill, they
heard a sound. There in a tree was a blackbird
singing a lovely song - as always.

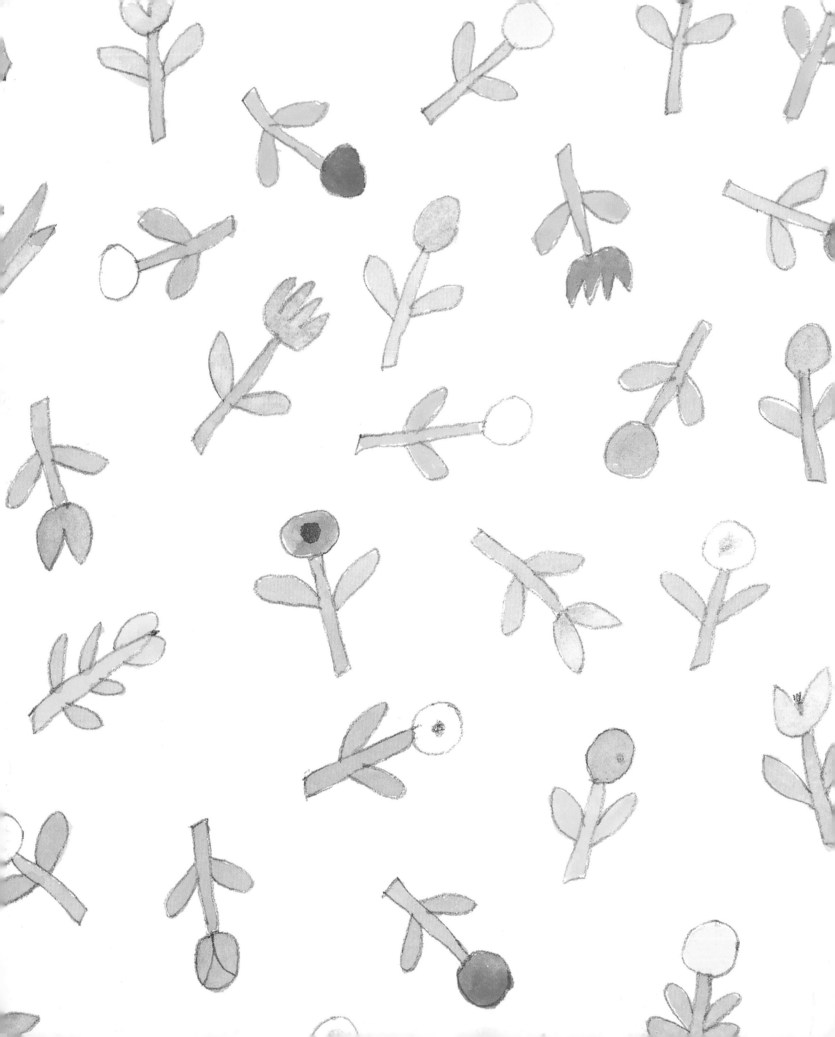

Max Velthuijs's twelve beautiful stories about **Frog** and his friends first started to appear twenty five years ago and are now available as paperbacks, e-books and apps.

9781783441440   9781783441532   9781783441501   9781783441426

9781783441471   9781783441457   9781783441525   97811783441433

9781783441518   9781783441495   9781783441488   9781783441419

Max Velthuijs (Dutch for Field House) lived in the Netherlands, and received the prestigious Hans Christian Andersen Medal for Illustration. His charming stories capture childhood experiences while offering life lessons to children as young as three, and have been translated into more than forty languages.

'**Frog is an inspired creation — a masterpiece of graphic simplicity.**' **GUARDIAN**

'**Miniature morality plays for our age.**' **IBBY**